James Patriot Wilson

In memoriam - John P. Jackson Jr.

James Patriot Wilson

In memoriam - John P. Jackson Jr.

ISBN/EAN: 9783744756181

Printed in Europe, USA, Canada, Australia, Japan

Cover: Foto ©Raphael Reischuk / pixelio.de

More available books at **www.hansebooks.com**

IN MEMORIAM.

———

John P. Jackson, Jr.

———

Born February 6th, A.D. 1857.
Died December 17th, A.D. 1889.

THIS MEMORIAL was prepared at the request of the friends of the late MR. JACKSON, and contains the memorial delivered at the funeral by the Rev. James P. Wilson, D.D.; a record of the action taken by the Courts and the Bar, and the proceedings at the anniversary of the Class of 1856, at Princeton College, upon the announcement of his death, together with other tributes of affection and respect.

The funeral services were held at the family homestead, on the corner of Kinney and High streets, Newark, N. J., on December 24, 1880.

After the singing of the hymn "Asleep in Jesus," the Rev. Dr. Wilson read portions of the Scriptures from Corinthians, XV, and Revelation, XXI and XXII. The memorial address was followed by a prayer from the Rev. J. F. Stearns, D. D. After the singing of the hymn, "Brief Life is here our Portion," the Benediction was pronounced, and the last mortal remains were interred in Mount Pleasant Cemetery, the following gentlemen officiating as pall bearers: Judge D. A. Depue, Henry Young, J. Henry Stone, E. H. Wright, D. A. Ryerson, E. R. Pennington, F. N. Torrey, A. Kirkpatrick, A. P. Whitehead, S. P. Stearns.

MEMORIAL ADDRESS

DELIVERED BY

Rev. JAMES P. WILSON, D.D.,

PASTOR OF THE SOUTH PARK PRESBYTERIAN CHURCH, NEWARK, N. J.

Nineteen years and eight days ago the lifeless form of
JOHN P. JACKSON, Esq., was borne out of that door
to the vehicle waiting to convey him to his last resting-
place,—a man of wonderful activities and Christian
energy, greatly missed and beloved and deeply lamented. His place is not yet filled, even to this day.

Fourteen years after that, October 18th, 1875, another beautiful life went out in this home—a lovely
and most beloved woman. We never shall forget
seeing her body carried out by her five stalwart, manly
sons, bearing their mother across that threshold to lay
her beside the husband of her youth. The best possible testimony to the parental fidelity, the conscientious
training and the cheerful and consistent example of
the united head of this household is seen in the fact that
of the large family sorrowing there—and they are all
here, except this one who lies before us, "first fruits,"
who has gone to the reunion in Heaven—every one of

them is a member of the Church of Christ without a
single exception. No better testimony could by any
possibility be given to the pure life, the correct example,
the religious training and the tender instruction of those
who thus so nobly fulfilled life's most solemn responsi-
bility. And now we are here at the funeral of one of
the family who will likewise be carried out for burial.
The "first fruits," as I said a moment ago, the first
one gone to form that certain reunion which will take
place before many years; when they all shall be gathered, an entire circle, we doubt not, by God's grace will
be complete.

JOHN P. JACKSON, JR., who lies before us, was born
February 6th, 1837. His early school days were passed
in this city, under competent instruction. In 1856 he
graduated at Princeton College, in a class in which
were some very distinguished men, among whom,
with others, it is enough for me only to mention the
name of the REV. DR. DURYEA, now of Boston. MR.
JACKSON took the first honor of his class; he then
went to the universities of Yale and Harvard, and
there pursued the study of law, and returned to this
city to engage in the practice of his profession. It is
not necessary to pursue at any great length this part
of his earthly record, for his life is before us all. You
have seen him going in and out, and have marked his
integrity and his bright example in all those beautiful
qualities that adorn our common human nature. Who
can ever forget the genial grasp of his hand, the kin

dling eye, the frank, gentle deportment that always characterized him: high or low, black or white made no difference, he had a warm shake of the hand for every one. It is difficult to conceive of a death in this city under any circumstances that could make such an impression as the death of our beloved friend lying before us. It is just as if a rifle shot had taken him from the head of his pew at South Park Church, so sudden and unlooked-for was his departure,—and yet though so sudden, perfectly safe, as we have reason to believe. Some things can be repaired, lost crowns and sceptres may be regained, the flush of youth may be renewed, the pallid countenance resume the hue of health, and vigor once more return to the emaciated frame—even a tarnished reputation may be made good by a life of consecrated energy and devotion—but who can replace the treasures rent from our bleeding, broken hearts by the ruthless hand of the great destroyer, Death? What equivalent from this life can make amends for such a deprivation? What deeds of heroic self-denial, ministries of mercy, capabilities of sympathy, and of willing self-denial known only to the Omniscient, aspirations, influences potent for blessings, pleadings for the true, achievements, potentialities, active, exhausting, self-relying, and yet so greatly uplifting to us all—all these and much more lie now within that casket soon to be closed and committed to the earth. But who of all this company here believes that this is the end of it? Is life a mere dumb show ? Is there nothing beyond the cold stream of death, and when this brief, fitful earthly existence is over is there nothing further ? Who believes this ?

We are under the law. That law is the law of our Maker, written in the very nature of man himself. From our relation to God, we are bound to love and trust and serve and obey Him. To neglect this is revolt and must involve misery. The perfections of Deity, the capacity of our souls, and our absolute dependence make this fact certain. It is not a mere arbitrary enactment, and the revealed moral law of our Sovereign is only, after all, a republication of this law of nature originally in man's soul. This is what gives death his sting and imparts to him his power. The ancients knew nothing about death. Their poets and orators and philosophers had no remedy and did not know what to say about death ; they reared altars to every virtue and to every vice, but never yet has there been found an altar reared to death. They felt that they could not propitiate death ; all they could say was, that it was inevitable, and nothing more. The Stoics had only some faint, obscure hints of an immortal life hereafter, and the Platonists' ideas are but little more than a poetic fancy after all ; and Aristotle, the wisest and most subtle of all the ancient philosophers, admitted that "of all the terrible things in this world, death was the most terrible."

Now, if death was such a terrible thing to the heathen, what must it be to men in a Christian land who know something of God in his perfections, and feel themselves under law conscious violators, and therefore are obnoxious to the penalty? It is through Christ alone we now have an idea of immortality,—but immortality alone confers no boon since that consciousness of being sinners against God which every man has makes death a terror to us all. Through the Lord Jesus Christ, life and immortality have been brought to light, and we now have positive proof of it in his resurrection from the grave. No man proved the natural immortality of the human soul : the analogies of nature and the presumptions of reason are strong, but they are not conclusive. But we have now authentic proof in the fact that Jesus Christ went down into the darkness of the grave and came back with the wreath of victory on his marble brow, and gives immortal life to all those who follow Him. He took away all the uncertainty of the future world, and the Christian now, in bidding farewell to the long-cherished associations of this human life, and to the things that attract and enslave our hearts here, has a glorious home-bringing when he dies. He goes to his Father's house and at once enters on the realization of all his highest conceptions.

What takes place immediately on dissolution we know not. We confess that sometimes the most intense curiosity is awakened to get a glimpse of the opening glories of that second life beyond the stars, but the communication would probably be as incomprehensible

to us **as it is** unprofitable. Suppose we could tell the
caterpillar that it would be a butterfly, and rise to another existence entirely different from that which it
previously had, and sport in the air and glow and glit-
ter in the sunbeam of the heavens. Or suppose some
one could have told you and me, before we came into
this world, what it was to **be**, with **all** its new and
amazing scenes, its science and art, its hopes, its ex-
periences of joy and grief, its progressive **life**, its epi-
sodes of tenderness, its affections in their endless vari-
ety and beauty and their infinite hope, we never could
have believed it. Just **so** I believe it **will be** when we
cross the **river of** death. It gives **us a** most intense
curiosity **to** know what takes place after death. We
shall be conscious, no doubt, of vitality more than we
dream of here, even such that the word *life* will seem
never before to have had any meaning. But we want
more—not immortality only, which of itself is no
boon—but **we** want *forgiveness*. We are conscious of
sin. Nature can testify to many **divine** attributes—to
God's power and wisdom and goodness. The evidence
of these are around us everywhere in creation.

But she has not one **word about** forgiveness. **Her**
laws, so far as we can know, run **in a** contrary direc-
tion. Crime perpetrated **can** never **be** set right. A
man may die in agonies of remorse for past transgres-
sions, but he cannot rectify one which he has once
committed. Tears of contrition are unavailing. The
sigh of broken-hearted penitence breathed in secret is

of no avail. Nature knows of no mercy for an of-
fender. She presses her finger to her lips and main-
tains perfect silence. The Lord Jesus Christ tells us
we are forgiven. But we want even more than this.
We must be loved and taken to the bosom of infinite
paternal tenderness. Jesus gives me that precious
promise, and assures me that I am united to Him
by a tie than which there can be nothing stronger.
Not merely an identity of interest and sympathy, but
a part of the Redeemer's own body, and if there is a
stronger union I know not what it is. Such a union
is that between us and Christ, and as Augustine said,
"where the head is, there all the members must be,"
and where the Lord Jesus is, thither we shall follow
and we shall all be there. Oh ! then, say nothing to me
about mere morality, about man fulfilling all the duties
of common life around him, in its ever-varied relations,
and on this ground resting a hope of heaven. You
are beginning at the wrong end. Have your fellow-
men claims that you cannot and dare not ignore, and
has Almighty God no claim ?—He who made you and
redeemed you, and whose daily mercies and blessings
are strewn around your path in every step of your going
through life ? All these moral duties must be done,
and not leave the other and higher undone. We insist
upon it, that the same love of excellences which
appears to manifest itself in every form of creative
goodness shall be just as evident in the relations which
we sustain to Him who demands from us, on every

ground, the highest love of which the human heart is
capable. Is there any extravagance in demanding for
God a regard as definite, as vivid in its personal consciousness, as marked in all its natural evidences, as any
human affection can call forth? Is gratitude due to one's
fellow-men in return for favors received at their hands,
and shall our infinite debt to our Maker remain unac-
knowledged and **unpaid**, and no warm emotion **fill**
and overflow our hearts?

But let us test this claim **of love to** supreme excellence and see how **it stands. It will** always be at-
tracted to the character that seems to possess most **of**
it. Personal affection for another will always desire
the happiness of the object of such affection. **It** will
study the wishes of the one beloved and comply with
them when absent, or even when they are **no** longer
living. "If ye **love** me, keep my commandments."
True love ever demands responsive return, and cannot
rest and be calm if unloved. It pants for God's love,
and it must have some communion with the object **of**
affection. We love the *society* of those whom we love.
These are some tests, and there have been in all ages
men who have said that these were their feelings
toward the Author of their being—the Supreme **ob**-
ject of their worship. Let these few tests be applied
to that morality which some plead for their acceptance
with the final Judge, and the utter insufficiency will
appear.

We come, then, to-day **and** stand beside this coffin

and here see the triumph of Christian faith. To the excellence of his public character abundant testimony has already been given. Of what he was in private life I shall say nothing : within these sacred precincts strangers are not allowed to enter. None may intrude upon the privacy of domestic joys and sorrows. I can speak only from the knowledge of others. But it was a Christian life and Christian household : a life of prayer and systematic effort and devotion in doing good to the children God had given him. Of what he was in the church, in the Sunday-school, and in the prayer-meeting I am fully competent to speak. I could not but remark, in conversation with a friend two or three months ago, that it seemed to me John P. Jackson was ripening for another world. I could not but notice an increasing depth of tone in his Christian life and a manful gentleness and candor and purity in all his social intercourse. I knew him personally, and I think I knew him intimately, and I never heard him speak ill of a human being, and could not but remark, with many others, the uniform kindness with which he spoke of his fellow-men, and the generous construction which he was ever ready to put upon their opinions and upon all their actions.

But he has passed away and gone to a brighter and better world. That eye will kindle on earth no more with affection, that voice no more be heard, nor the warm grasp of his hand be felt. The sun, the soft breeze, the " fierce autumnal rain " will fall alike unheeded upon him. He is done with earth, has cast away its heavy chain. Let me here read a brief extract from a writing found among his papers after his death. I read it because of its interest as eminently descriptive of his own life, the latter part especially :

" Then comes the great practical difficulty, how to live. We are seduced by desires for wealth as well as by the heresies of unbelief. The '*flesh-pots of Egypt*' are powerful, as well as the seductions of culture. Now we must be diligent, industrious, ingenious, but we must also be contented, happy if possible, cheerful, not too ambitious or proud, least of all envious : make the most of our advantages, but not envy or repine. Aim at gentle and loving dispositions, and to foster the same in our children and friends. Try to help others in every incidental way. Study the laws of physical health and of business success. But most and principally keep the soul so in tune with the spirit of its Divine Creator that it will early betake itself to Him at all times in life, and readily find its place in His bosom at the close of an earthly existence."

I have recited but a portion of the manuscript. A part of the paper had a date, but the extract I have just read had none. I think his life was founded on that model, and could a human life be directed by better principles? I have no doubt it was his own ideal, and nobly did he carry it out. Mr. Jackson was in the forty-fourth year of his age. The active men of Newark are just about that age, and who can say " it may not be his turn next." It is a most significant warning. The human voice amounts to nothing when God speaks as he does in this providence to-day. You will pass out from these sad scenes into the world. The vanities of life, its distractions, cares and necessary pursuits will lead you astray, but you have yet to come to the hour when the curtains will be drawn around your bed, and your friends speak in whispers as they draw near, and you will know from the anxious countenance of your physician that your end is nigh. Then, oh! then, in that dread crisis, when your spirit is about to plume its wings for an everlasting flight, nothing but religion will bear up your fainting soul, nothing but to be able to say, " My Redeemer is mine and I am His," " I know whom I have believed," " They call, I follow to a land unknown; I trust in Thee and know in whom I trust."

Oh, my friends, will you pardon me if I express to-day a hope that you will not longer postpone this great work of loving Christ as your Saviour, and then in life's last and darkest hour will come the breaking day, the light of conscious reconciliation, the peace, the love of God, will dawn on the confiding soul, and continue to shine upon it forever. And to God the Father, Son and Holy Ghost be all the praise and glory forever. Amen.

The REV. DR. STEARNS offered the following prayer :

Lord, Thou hast been our dwelling place in all generations. Before the mountains were brought forth, or ever Thou didst

from **the earth** or the world, from everlasting to everlasting,
Thou art God. Thou turnest man from destruction and say-
est, "Return, ye children of men," and Thou art teaching us
not only from Thy holy word, but by the admonitions of Thy
providence, that we have no continuing city here, and cannot
tell what a day may bring forth; but we know that if the
Lord is on our side then we are prepared to live or to die, to
suffer or to rejoice, as may seem best in Thy wise and holy eye.
Unto Thee, O Lord our God, we come at this sorrowful moment to ask of Thee Thy consolation; unto Thee, the Father
of our spirits, who, as a father pitieth his children, doth pity
them that fear Him, unto Thee, blessed Saviour, who didst
come to comfort them that mourn; unto Thee, Spirit of all
truth and all consolation, beseeching Thee to uphold and guide
and cheer us, and to sanctify to us the sting through which
we are called to pass. O Lord, Thou art reminding us that
we are born to die, that in the midst of life we are in death,
that we know not what a day may bring forth. Give us
grace, we pray Thee, so as to profit by this sign, this admonition of Thy holy providence, that we shall have occasion to
say as we look back, "It is good for us that God our Father
has chastened us. We come to Thee to commend to Thee
these mourners, with whose sorrow no stranger intermeddleth,
but which Thou canst understand and Thou canst so sanctify
that it shall work out a far more exceeding and eternal meas-
ure of glory. O Thou, who art the father of the fatherless
and the God of the widow, draw near, we pray Thee, at this
sorrowful hour to her from whom Thou hast taken away by
this sudden stroke the husband of her youth, upon whom she
has leaned for support, who has cheered her from day to day by
his love and by his cheerfulness; he whom she leaned upon as
her support for all future years of life. O Lord, our God,
Thou knowest the sorrow that pervades that heart, and all we
can do is to commend her to Thee and the word of Thy grace,
which is able to build her up and give her inheritance among

all those that are sanctified. Take these bereaved children
under Thy care, shield them from all the perils of their or-
phanage and be Thou more than ever a father to them since
Thou hast taken their earthly father, as we trust, to Thyself.
We thank Thee, O Lord our God, for all he was permitted to
do for them while he was here upon the earth. We thank Thee
for the principles that have been instilled in their young and
tender lives; let them be permanent, and let them strengthen
as they go on upon the journey of life and into life's tempta-
tions, and may they all be spared to do worthy things here on
earth, to exert a good influence, and then to go and join him
who has gone before and form an unbroken family in those
mansions which Christ has gone to prepare. We commend to
Thee, Father of all mercies, that mother who knows not yet
the bereavement she has been called upon to bear ; be with
her wherever she is, preserve her from all the perils to which
her distant journey is exposed, and bring her safely home to
this sorrowing daughter and family in Thine own good time.
And do Thou, O Lord, bless every member of this numerous
family circle, brothers, sisters and friends, and give them
the consolation which the world cannot give or take away.
Thou hast not stricken them for a long time. Thou hast permitted them to share each other's joys and sorrows from day
to day, and we thank Thee for the past and pray that Thou
wilt more than make up to them this loss by the rich com-
munications of Thy spirit. O Thou who was with the father
and mother in days long gone by, remember, we pray Thee,
their prayers; remember the counsels they left behind them
to their children and their children's children, and in all the
generations that succeed we pray that there may be a purpose
to serve the God of their fathers. We pray, O Father in
Heaven, that Thou wilt impress this lesson Thou art giving
us on all gathered together here; on all those who knew and
loved our departed friend; upon those who were associated
with him in his profession, upon those who were accustomed

to mingle in society with him, who will miss his warm hand-shake, and his cordial words and tones; we pray that Thou wilt so enable them to profit by this lesson Thou art giving them that it shall tend to their greater usefulness while they continue here in the world, for their more rapid advancement in every worthy attainment and for their everlasting salvation in Thy heavenly kingdom. We pray Thee, O Lord, that Thou wilt sanctify this affliction to the church of which our beloved friend has been so long an honored and efficient member. We thank Thee for all he has been able to do there in the building up of the church in the faith and power of the Gospel of Christ, in strengthening the hands of its pastor and encouraging his heart. And now we pray Thee that Thou wilt comfort this bereaved family with those consolations which the world cannot give nor take away, and may this admonition of Thy holy providence be made an instrument of Thy hands in bringing all the members of the church of Christ into closer fellowship and Christian love, and in bringing into the fold of Jesus any who are standing without, without hope and without God, in the world. O Lord, our God, Thou art speaking to us all. Thou art saying to us all, who knew and loved our departed friend, "Be ye also ready, for in such an hour as ye think not the Son of Man cometh." O Lord, we cannot tell how soon our call may come. We would stand with our loins girded about us and with our lights burning and we ourselves as those who wait for the coming of the Lord, that when he cometh and knocketh we may open immediately. Oh, let not death take any of us by surprise, but may it find all of us ready and may we be prepared to say, "Lord, now lettest Thou Thy servant depart in peace according to Thy word, for mine eyes have seen Thy salvation." Go with us, we pray Thee, as we go to deposit the lifeless form of our departed friend in the place appointed for all, guide all our meditations, help us to lay to heart the lessons Thou hast given us in Thy holy providence, and when we return to the active duties of life, may it be with new self-consecration to Thee, and to live as becomes disciples of Christ and children of the Heavenly Father, discharging every duty of this life and growing in grace and in the knowledge of our Lord and Saviour, and preparing for that rest which remains for the people of God. Hear us, O Lord, and answer us, for Jesus' sake, and Thine be all the praise for ever and ever. Amen.

The hymn, " Brief life is here our portion," was then sung, after which the Rev. Dr. Wilson pronounced the benediction. The remains were conveyed to Mount Pleasant Cemetery for interment.

October 2d, 1880.

General concession—that beliefs or **mere** creeds are modified—some shaking off of old statements—departure of some *orthodox* denominations from the ancient standards of Westminster Catechism, although Presbyterians certainly, in theory, maintain the **old** theology.

Yet along with these changes, the same hopes, fears and necessities exist. **Men** cannot get along still without some religion; they cannot endure a mere blank; the mere *culture* or *intellectual appreciation* of the best things in life is not enough, certainly not enough for the great masses of humanity, who cannot expect much culture, and among the most cultured we know it **is** awfully unsatisfactory—and the great element of *soul* is common to all men and it has its demands to make and relationship to sustain, and it even still is either the uncomfortable monitor, constantly roughening the would-be smooth action of our other forces, or it is the gentle, but strong and ungovernable spirit which bears us safely through all adversity and trial and keeps us at home with ourselves and with God.

As practical men is it not best to conclude that it is wisest for us to occupy our minds with soul cultivation rather than brooding over contested points of theology. About certain facts no Christian church can differ: (1) That Christ died; (2) the magnitude of the sacrifice shows both the existence of enormous guilt and sin and also the grandeur and comprehensiveness of the result. Having got so far, is it not the next proposition that we not only ought to give an acceptance of all the teachings of this Christ, involving the study of His word and the following of His example, and this will serve, if anything will, to keep our spirits (souls) in unison with His—working as He worked—and prepared for an easy transition from this world to the next.

This sort of soul-culture is so simple that it is adapted to all mankind, universal in its application. Its results are far more cheering and satisfactory than the agnostic system of culture, and better prepares one for every-day life; but does it not also imply a simplicity of belief instead of a dreary mystification of metaphysics—does it not ignore such disputes as concern predestination or any other hindrances to universal salvation? Does it not banish too severe introspection and constant criticising of motives by the broad and general assumption that, for better or worse, in our trying to live like Christ and become His followers because we believe in Him and don't believe in ourselves, and therefore are not concerned with making ourselves perfect. This introspection, however, besides being uncertain and depressing, seems sometimes to proceed on the idea that we can make ourselves chaste and perfect thereby! a great fallacy. Very little introspection is taught in the Bible—it is rather— looking upwards.

2

Then comes the great practical difficulty, how to live. **We**
are seduced by desires for wealth, as well as by the heresies of
infidelity. The *flesh-pots of Egypt* are powerful, as well as
the seduction of culture. Now, we must be diligent, industrious, ingenious, but we **must also** be contented, happy if
possible, cheerful, and not too ambitious or proud, least of all
envious. Make the most of our advantages, but not envy or
repine. Aim at gentle and loving dispositions and to foster
the same in our children and friends. Try **to** help others in
every incidental way. Study the laws **of** physical health and
business success; but most and principally keep the soul so
in tune with the spirit of its divine Creator that it will easily
betake itself to Him at all times in life and readily find its
place in His bosom at the close of our earthly existence.

MEMORIAL TRIBUTES.

[*Daily Advertiser, December 22d.*]

IN MEMORIAM.

JOHN P. JACKSON, ENTERED INTO REST DECEMBER 17, 1880.

We know not why—ofttimes the reaper dread
His rightful harvest passes by, and leaves
Untouched the ripened grain and golden sheaves,
While at his summons beauty bows the head,
And youth and manhood's prime are captive led.

We know not why—we only know that one
Who yesterday among us went and came,
Bearing in honor still an honored name,
A strong man among men, his race hath run,
And God hath willed it so—His will be done.

We know not why—we see but darkly here;
And we shall mourn and miss the kindly face,
The stalwart form replete with manly grace,
The hearty greeting and the words of cheer,
And long shall hold his name and memory dear.

We know not why—hereafter we shall know;
Then peace and rest; for while glad bells at morn
Ring in the day on which the Christ was born,
And from afar our tears and prayers must flow,
His ravished eyes, Oh, wondrous depth of grace,
Shall see a risen Saviour face to face.

                                        T. B.

[*Daily Advertiser, December 20th.*]

The Rev. Dr. Wilson, of the South Park Presbyterian Church, yesterday morning preached a sermon appropriate to the death of John P. Jackson, Jr., from Job xxvii., 18. In the afternoon, at a meeting of the Missionary Union of the church, David C. Dodd, Jr., presiding, the following resolutions, offered by John Y. Foster, and seconded by A. L. Bassett and George W. **Howell**, were adopted:

The officers and **teachers of** the Sunday-schools of **the** South Park Presbyterian Church, having learned with **profound** sorrow of the sudden decease of their fellow-laborer, John P. Jackson, Jr., desire to put upon record, in this formal expression, their cordial appreciation of his character and work as a Christian, and their testimony to his usefulness and zeal in all departments of religious effort. Earnest in **his** convictions, conscientious in his performance of duty, loyal to every essential moral principle, obedient alike to the stimulus and to the restraint of high motive, doing with exceptional cheerfulness and alacrity whatever was demanded of him in the sphere of Christian activity, his example constituted a potential force in this church and community, and while we mourn his unexpected departure, we rejoice that in his life and the recollection of its manliness, its uprightness and its many Christ-like fruits, we have a compensation for this present loss which is at once an inspiration and a solace. Cut down in the bloom of manhood and the maturity of its powers, he speaks to us from his coffin to-day: "Be ye also ready, with loins girt—along the Lord's work faithfully and untiringly—for in such an hour as you think not he may call you also."

At a meeting of the Board of Trustees of the South Park Presbyterian Church, held this 20th day of December, 1880, the following preamble and resolutions were unanimously adopted:

WHEREAS, Having learned with unfeigned sorrow of the sudden death of our esteemed associate and friend, the late JOHN P. JACKSON, JR., for many years a member of this Board; and

WHEREAS, In the all-wise dispensation of our Heavenly Father, by which he was so suddenly removed from earthly friends and associates; and while we sorrow not as those without hope, but believing " that not even a sparrow falls to the ground without our Heavenly Father"; and as the dispensation now seems, it is made light only by faith in an unseen world, and through a helpful, loving Saviour; therefore be it

Resolved, That while we bow submissively to the will of Divine Providence in this affliction, we would desire to place on record, on the minutes of this Board, our high appreciation of his sterling qualities of heart and life, his genial temperament, his active interest in all things pertaining to the prosperity of this church, his sincere desire for the well-being of all, and his Christian character and life.

Resolved, That a copy of these resolutions be published in the daily newspapers of this city, and also presented to his bereaved family.

PROCEEDINGS OF ESSEX COUNTY BAR.

On the morning of Saturday, December 18th, 1880, Judge Depue announced to the Court the death of JOHN P. JACKSON, JR. He said :

The Court has seen in the paper this morning the announcement of the death of one of the members of the Bar, MR. JOHN P. JACKSON, JR., and the Court deems it its duty, on its own motion, at this, the first session after that sad event, to take some notice of the death of MR. JACKSON. It is a duty that, to me personally, is painful. He was one of my earliest acquaintances after I came to Newark, and from that time till the close of his life I had experienced from him the greatest kindness. Our associations had been of the pleasantest and most agreeable character. The Court will officially announce the death of MR. JACKSON, and the adjournment of the Court out of respect to his memory, and at the request of the members of the Bar, will announce that a meeting of the Bar will be held on some day early next week for the purpose of enabling its members to give a proper expression of their feelings on this subject. I may add, with a view to the business of the Court during the coming week, that when the date of the funeral shall be announced there will be no session of the Court on that day. The members of the Bar will have an opportunity to hold a meeting in this Court-room on that morning, and after that meeting the Court will be adjourned for the day. The Clerk will please enter the order of the Court on the minutes.

In pursuance of the call of Judge Depue, the Essex County Bar met at the Court-house in the City of Newark on the morning of Tuesday, the 21st day of December.

It was announced by Mr. William A. Righter that the Clerk had received a letter from Judge Depue, stating that it was impossible for him to be present and therefore he would move that Hon. Amzi Dodd be requested to take the chair.

The motion was approved, and Judge Dodd having taken the chair. Mr. George S. Duryee was appointed secretary of the meeting.

On motion of Mr. Charles A. Borcherling, that the Chair appoint a committee to draw up suitable resolutions commemorative of the death of JOHN P. JACKSON, JR., the following gentlemen were appointed as such committee: Mr. J. Henry Stone, Mr. Cortlandt Parker, Mr. Thomas N. McCarter, Mr. William A. Righter, and Mr. Caleb S. Titsworth.

THE CHAIRMAN then said:

GENTLEMEN OF THE BAR — I greatly regret the absence of Judge Depue, who was expected to preside on this occasion. It is unnecessary for me to state the object which has convened us this morning — the very unexpected and lamentable death of our friend, Mr. JACKSON, the

circumstances of which have already been made public,
and which are well understood by all the members of
the Bar. We are met now to take such suitable action
in regard to this lamentable event as may be dictated by
the feelings and judgment of the members of the Bar,
and we are ready now, and will be glad, to hear any
expression which members of this meeting may be disposed
to make in regard to it.

MR. HENRY YOUNG said :

MR. CHAIRMAN — Nearly five years have elapsed since
our brotherhood assembled thus, in solemn meeting, to
mourn the loss of the lamented Perry. He had just entered
upon a career of successful professional life, and was stricken
down in the midst of his work. Again, to-day, we lament
the loss of another gallant knight, who, with his armor on,
has fallen honorably in the front ranks of the battle.

To us the death of JOHN P. JACKSON brings a sense of
personal loss. He was my intimate friend, and I fear that
the tribute of affection and personal worth which I would
utter may fail, through grief, to find proper expression.

But of whom was he not the faithful and just friend?
His noble heart and generous disposition included all who
were worthy of a good man's friendship. Hence, the great
public shock. Our expression of sorrow is not—cannot be
—merely conventional. It is the offering of affectionate
love and kind remembrance, in which this large community
regretfully joins.

MR. CHAIRMAN — We are confronted once more with the
mystery of our existence. This man, who seemed physically
so strong, and intellectually gave promise of such continued
future usefulness, has suddenly and unexpectedly fallen

out of our ranks. If, on the opening day of this term of
Court, at which Mr. Jackson was present, a question had
suggested itself as to which one of us all here should, in
the customary ordering of events, be first called to answer
the summons of the King of Terrors, no one's thought
would have dwelt for an instant upon our friend's death as
probable in the near future. His handsome face and mag-
nificent physique suggested at once the best health and
greatest vitality. And so accustomed are we to associate in
our thoughts the promise of future usefulness with its
development — so great is the world's need of good, intelligent young men — that the loss of one such always seems
inexplicable, mysterious — almost unjust. Why it is that
this man, before others — this strong man — should have
fallen, we cannot tell. His death furnishes another
mystery of life. We can only say that this result
expresses the inscrutable will of a wise and kind Supreme
Ruler. If it shall arrest our heedless thought, and direct
it to a future life, however sorrowful it may be, it will
not be entirely in vain to us.

Mr. Jackson's life was short, but eminently successful
and complete. If, without effort at analysis, we judge of
it only by its results, it seems very noble and harmonious.

In his early school-life he was the pupil of the late
Nathan Hedges, than whom a better instructor in those
studies now regarded as preliminary probably never lived.
Thence he went, in preparation for college, to the Phillips
Academy, a school of national repute, then under the wise
control of the late Dr. Samuel H. Taylor. Having com-
pleted his course of studies there, he entered Princeton
College, and graduated from that institution in 1856 at
the head of his class. His class in college had in it
several young men then and since distinguished for

studious habits and fine scholarship. He was easily first,
and came forth from the curriculum full of physical
energy and mental vigor, realizing the desirable result of
a sound mind in a sound body, and furnishing in this
respect a marked contrast to most first-honor men.

It is worthy of remark that his father, years before,
had gained the same honorable distinction in the same
institution of learning.

I remember well the Commencement Exercises at
Princeton in 1859. I had just been admitted into the
Sophomore class, and was entering upon my college life.
MR. JACKSON had been selected to deliver at that time
the master's oration, which, as the Chairman well knows,
is delivered by a member of each class three years after
graduation. This selection is made by the Faculty of the
college, and is determined by a regard to oratorical gifts
as well as good scholarship. The choice was, hence, a
mark of distinction, and MR. JACKSON's oration more
than justified this appointment. I recollect distinctly
— as do others here, no doubt — how his vigorous and
thoughtful eloquence and fine manly appearance impressed
the great and critical audience that was assembled on that
occasion.

After graduation, he entered the law office of Joseph P.
Bradley, now a Justice of the Supreme Court of the
United States, then engaged in the practice of his
profession in this city. During his clerkship here, he
attended lectures at, and graduated from, the Dane Law
School, at Cambridge, Massachusetts, an institution from
which have come forth some of the best lawyers the
country has produced. I remember a remark made by
the late Emory Washburn, the eminent author of the
treatises on Easements and Real Property, and then a

Professor in that institution, that the Princeton boys were among the best students who came to the school; and I remember, also, that he frequently spoke to me — for he was a man of genial manners and easy approach — in the highest terms of our friend JACKSON. How well he deserved this praise is shown by the fact that while in the Law School he secured the first prize which was offered for the best legal essay. The competition was voluntary, but many entered the lists.

Thus equipped for his profession, he entered manfully upon its pursuits. He brought to it a mind imbued with high professional sentiment, love for learning, and recognition of integrity as essential to advancement. In these respects his mind was the natural product of his birth and education, for few men have had better home advantages than he.

Early in his professional life he became the partner of our friend ex-Senator Stone, and entered upon a successful practice.

He was for several years Counsel for the City of Newark; he was twice elected to the House of Assembly of this State by one of the most intelligent constituencies of the State, and during his second term received the honorary nomination for Speaker of the House, his party being then in the minority. He was also, for many years, counsel in this county for one of the largest corporations of this State, and but one year ago was appointed by the Governor as one of a Commission to draft a general tax law for the State, a task which required the highest legal attainments. He has filled other and honorable professional positions, and in all has earnestly, faithfully and honestly discharged his duties.

But no mere recognition of his high merits as a

lawyer compasses his character. Of him it may be said
more truly than of most men that all those qualities
which go to make a marked man were combined in his
constitution. His character was symmetrical. He filled
well all relations of life. As a citizen he was public-
spirited and intelligent, always ready to lend his time and
voice and talent to the discussion and solution of public
questions.

In his intercourse with his fellow-men he was essentially
a courteous gentleman; in this respect, too, none named
him but to praise him. The poor, the obscure, the
humble remember to-day his kindly greeting and hearty
recognition. In social circles he was pre-eminent. He
was the life of such gatherings, and the joyousness of his
disposition and the exuberance of his spirits, combined
with marked civility and politeness, made him always a
welcome guest and warm-hearted host. How kind he was
to his friends, how thoughtful of their wishes and
happiness, how anticipative of their pleasure, none but
those who knew him intimately can tell. He was a pure-
minded man. I have known him intimately for years,
and never during my intercourse with him have I known
him to utter a thought that could not be freely expressed
in the most sensitive circle.

Thus learned and successful in his profession, of great
public spirit and intelligence, courteous and polite to all,
amiable in manner and disposition to a marked degree, our
friend possessed, also, that other grace of mind and living
which is essential to a perfect character. He was an
earnest, unassuming Christian gentleman. At church, at
the Sunday-school, at the weekly religious meetings, he
was a constant attendant; and not an attendant merely —
he was a worker, and content to be a worker in the

ranks. His faith was simple and unquestioning. He had realized in his life the truth of Von Humboldt's saying: "Into the Kingdom of God, as into the Kingdom of Nature, they who enter must become as little children."

But, Mr. Chairman, there are other more sacred relations of life where it is not permitted to us here to follow our dead friend. We cannot appropriately enter that desolate home, always heretofore bright and full of sunshine, where his wife and children mourn his untimely death. Nor can we speak here with propriety of that united band of noble brothers and sisters who lament his loss. Their grief, intense as it must be, is sacred.

Our friend JACKSON has passed away gently and quietly into that other world where "the wicked cease from troubling, and the weary are at rest." We have no fear for him. "All is well with him." We confidently believe that his spirit has ascended to a higher sphere of usefulness, and is still active and intelligent.

We will do well if we emulate the remarkable virtues, and follow in the footsteps of this young, brave, successful man, who has marked out for us all a life of true Christian living.

MR. CHARLES F. HILL then said:

MR. CHAIRMAN — It is not for me to attempt to improve on the eloquent words, and well-deserved words, of the gentleman who has just taken his seat, but I claim the privilege of paying to the memory of our departed friend a personal tribute. While it is an immeasurable loss to our profession — to the legal circle of this county — I feel myself that it is a personal loss to me. It is well known to the majority of the gentlemen present that I came into this city not long ago, an entire stranger, not having the acquaintance of a single member of the profession, and not having acquaintance among the laymen of this city even. I can never forget my relations with our departed friend. He was one of the first of the legal profession to whom I was introduced, and it has been a matter of gratitude with me during all these years as I have often remembered and thought of the efforts which were made by this Christian gentleman to make me feel that the gentlemen of the profession in Essex County would give me welcome to whatever position I could prove myself worthy of. I remember to-day with a great deal of gratitude, and with the deepest feeling, his efforts to make me feel that I was at home, that I was among friends; his frequent calls at my office when I was a stranger among a strange people, struggling for a position among you; his cheery words of encouragement; his manifestations of kindly friendship; his greeting upon the streets and in the public assemblies and wherever I met him, manifesting that degree of hospitality and of friendship which I have rarely ever met elsewhere; and I feel to-day that his death is a personal loss to me. And not only have I recognized him as a friend, but, as has been suggested by Mr. Young, I have been compelled to recognize him on all occasions in my associations with him as a true Christian man, as a man whose Christian character was rounded out and complete and beautiful; in all of my professional relations with him I have found that he carried his Christian principles, his high moral integrity, into his professional life — into his business life. I have found him always eminently a peacemaker; I have found him always to be an example for me wherever I have met him, and I can only say in closing that I mourn the loss of MR. JACKSON as a personal friend as well as a loss from our profession.

Mr. Edward M. Colie then said:

Mr. Chairman and Fellow-members of the Bar — It is, perhaps, more fitting that only those who, by reason of years, had a fuller acquaintance with Mr. Jackson than I had should speak on this occasion, but my heart will not permit me to remain silent. He was one of the gentlemen with whom I spent the student days of my life, before entering upon the practice of my profession: from him in part I gathered my first impression of legal ethics and received the encouragement and such helpful suggestions as were necessary to render pleasant and comparatively easy the work before me. Such was his vigor of life that when the news of his death came to me it impressed me with such a sense of improbability and such a sense of mystery that it seemed as if it must be the conjuring of some hideous dream: it was too sad to be a reality, even in this world of life and death. I never felt death brought so near to me as in this instance: so much of mystery seemed to enshroud it — so much of that which nobody can solve. The ancients, in the face of just such an appalling mystery as this, solved it by saying, "Whom the gods love die early," and the furthest we can reach to-day seems to be but little beyond that same solution, translating that language into Christian phrase, and saying, instead of "whom the gods love die early," this, "He giveth His beloved sleep." It is an overwhelming mystery, and it crowds upon me in such a way as to make my heart ache, not only for those who are grieving here, but for those inner circles to whom allusion has been so touchingly made.

I want to add what my heart forces me to say. I knew Mr. Jackson in relations somewhat different from those

in which most of you knew him. I knew him in the
office — in that part of professional life where, if anywhere,
characteristics and peculiarities are shown that are not read
of all men; where a man is seen in those relations by
which are developed qualities that detract from high
character; and I want to say here that during those three
years of student life, I cannot recall a single instance in
which my high appreciation of Mr. JACKSON's character,
morally and in every other respect, was in one degree
blemished, but, on the contrary — and not in that negative
form do I want to put it — his life in that office, amid
the perplexities and annoyances that will come to a busy
practitioner, was to me a guide and incentive and a clue
how to successfully, as far as in me lay, guide the life I
had to lead. I want, as I said before, to bear testimony
to the character of this inner circle of the professional life
of Mr. JACKSON, — to its purity, to its high moral tone,
to the example which it will be to me and to all who can
appreciate it in its fullness.

To me personally, Mr. JACKSON was a kind friend; to
me he gave those fruits of helpfulness that were so needed;
he was a kind counselor; his heart was always open
and his advice always willing in times of uncertainty and
perplexity, and within a few days, a little more than a
week ago, I had occasion, in that reliance, which I knew
was well placed, upon his kindness and his courtesy, to
approach him upon one of those subjects which come to a
young practitioner, where he needs the guidance and help
of those who are his seniors; and I found him as I always
found him, open, kind and glad to give to me the advice
that I needed and to help me over those rough places in
professional life where, being alone otherwise, my feet
might have slipped. Mr. JACKSON was a gentleman, as

has been said, and a Christian gentleman. He was a gentleman within that definition which surpasses all other definitions of a gentleman that I have ever found — the definition that came from the lips of the most courteous gentleman, perhaps, that ever lived, the poet warrior, Sir Philip Sidney, whose fame rests quite as much on his Christian courtesy and unselfishness on the field of battle, which led him to sacrifice, even when dying, his own comfort to appease the burning thirst of the wounded soldier at his side, as upon any deed of valor he wrought or any work of poetic beauty he ever conceived. He defined a gentleman as "one who hath high thoughts seated in a heart of courtesy." MR. JACKSON was a gentleman within that definition; his life was dominated by high thoughts and a noble ambition, and his heart was full to overflowing with the highest, truest courtesy.

MR. J. HENRY STONE (Chairman of the Committee on Resolutions), then said :

MR. CHAIRMAN — The Committee desire to report as follows :

"The announcement of the death of our brother, JOHN P. JACKSON, JR., strikes us with the shock of an unexpected blow. We know not why it is, when he had just fairly entered upon a career justifying the brilliant promises of his youth, he should so suddenly be required to lay aside all his hopes and leave us. We feel his loss with a sorrow that can come only from a personal affliction, and it is with sorrowful submission we recognize in it the hand of a Disposer whose power we cannot resist and whose wisdom we ought not to question.

3

" As a mark of regard for his memory, we, the members of the Essex County Bar, desiring to place upon record our great estimation of his worth, do therefore adopt the following minute:

" We feel a pride that our late brother was a member of our profession. We heartily attest his purity of life, his delicate sense of propriety, his conscientiousness to his clients, and his fidelity to all men.

" As a counselor, he added learning, dignity and respect to the Bar; as a companion, he furnished, beyond most others, the attractions of kindly courtesy and personal magnetism; as a man, he supplied something to the happiness of every one who knew him.

" In view of this lamented death, we tender our warmest sympathies to his bereaved family, and request the Court to have this minute made part of the Court records. We also request that a copy thereof be sent to his family and also to the Essex County Bar Association, of which he was an officer."

The committee likewise recommend the following:

" *Resolved*, That the Bar will meet here, and as a body attend his funeral, and that a copy of these proceedings be published in the journals of the city."

MR. CHAIRMAN — In asking the adoption of these resolutions, I feel emotions of no ordinary character. I had hoped to be present at the opening of this meeting, to announce the death of our friend, but was detained by a delay of the train, and I feel now such a deep sensibility of his loss that I do not know whether I ought to be

here. It seems to me that, with my feelings, I should
be better seen mourning with his family than present
here. I desire, however, to say something, though I am
not sure how I shall get on.

It seems to me as though we had just awakened from
the shock of what seemed to us a terrible dream, and
after all have found out it is not a dream. It was last
Saturday morning, when I was at Rahway, going to the
train, that I first heard the announcement of his death,
and it seemed to me that I hardly knew it before the
whole world appeared also to know it. People would
follow me in the streets on my road to the depot and
inquire about it. Passengers on the cars would come to
my seat to learn something of it. And when I arrived at
Newark, it seemed to me as though every one stopped me
to express his sorrow. In fact, these sad greetings were
so frequent that I came from my office to this Court-
room by an unusual route in order to avoid the pain of
meeting so many mourners who loved him.

Surely, Mr. Chairman, there must have been something
in him to have excited a sympathy so profound and so
extensive. I suppose that overpowering geniality of his,
which lifted you right into his current whether you wished
to get there or not, had a great deal to do with it. He
inherited from his mother, who was as nearly perfect as
any one could be, a disposition that was of as much
consequence to him as his education. He was an optimist
in a high sense. He took a cheerful view of everything
about him. He never met a person but what he seemed
to find something in him worth commending. I have
been intimate with him for half a generation. Except
when temporarily absent, there has never been a business

day when we were not together, and during all that time
he never addressed me with an unkind word. Only on
the rarest occasions have I heard him express unfriendly
opinions of any one. When most men do so, they follow
them up, stick to and defend them. He never cherished
such opinions; he could not help announcing them; but
after he had announced them, he left them alone to take
care of themselves. In addition to this, he had the very
rare faculty of being both a very good talker and a very
good listener; and he had an instinctive tact in moulding
the conversation in such form as to keep it attractive.
He had courage to defend his own views if attacked; but
if he thought they would beget difficulties, he preferred
not to aggressively announce them. His talk was always
sincere, but he insisted on making it pleasant. He
believed partly in the motto, "*Vera pro gratis*" but he
improved it by making it "*Vera et grata.*" And I think
this characteristic was one of his greatest charms. My
intimacy with him extends through occasions when we
have mingled our sorrows over the saddest calamities that
can happen to the living, and those in which we have
shouted our joys over hilarities that made us forgetful of
earth; yet between these wide extremes and during all
this long time, I never heard him use a word of deceit,
give expression to a coarse word or utter an impure
thought. Of his mental faculties I desire to say but
little. Able as they were, they were not of such a peculiar
or unusual character as to excite our interest so much as his
other qualities. He certainly had a good knowledge of
the science of law, and every day tried to add something
to it. In his legal and other intellectual pursuits his
mind was essentially conservative. I think original

research had little attraction for him. He was more
industrious to find a precedent than the reasoning of it
afterward. He believed the orthodox faith was approved
by the best and purest men. He agreed with them, and
adopted it without worrying over the quarrels about the
relationship of science to religion. While such minds
cannot be counted on in founding new sects or in creating
revolutions, they are, like his was, so entirely free from
all vagaries that their judgments are sound and eminently
reliable. He was politically somewhat ambitious, but he
was not very zealous in securing place. I think at one
time he would have been pleased with the appointment of
Law Judge for the county, and at another with the
nomination for Congress. Those are the only public
positions I ever heard him express a desire for, and I
know he would not have done one mean, importunate or
indelicate thing to have secured them ; and when they were
given to others the matter seemed to be easily forgotten.

But after all, it was not so much the intellectual or
political as the other traits of his character which gave to
it its chief charms. I never knew one who possessed
those other traits of which I have already spoken in such
an admirable degree, nor do I believe I shall ever know
such another.

And now, Mr. Chairman, he has left us to fight out
the rest of life's battles without him. For him we ought
not to mourn. If we are to be rewarded hereafter according to our conduct here, I am sure that God will see to
it that he is much better off than any one can be in life.
It is the loss to us here, it is the desolation that has
come to that home of his, that distresses us. It seems to
us such a cruel thing that she who has always lived in

the sunshine, who has never received scarcely **even a
sprinkle of sorrow,** should **so** suddenly **have** this **deluge**
poured over her, who knows too well, and over **those little**
ones, who know **nothing at all, as to what it means.**

We have, however, **sir, one** consolation; although **he
will not come back and again** add new life to **the atmosphere**
as he enters our doors with his enthusiastic presence, yet we
know that in a short time — and judging from his history
it may be very short — **we will** follow him. We **can at
least** indulge **in the hope that then we** shall meet him
again. I have a consciousness — if foolish, at least de-
lightful — that one **of** these days in the hereafter I shall
again meet his friendly grasp **and** cordial welcome; and
when, in a few hours, we shall bury all that is mortal of
him, my farewell salutation to **him** will **be the** words of
Tully: "**May** our **next** meeting give **us** much more
pleasure than this departure **gives us pain.**"

MR. CORTLANDT PARKER then said :

After listening **to one who** has **been able to repress his**
feelings **and** say a **few words so well,** perhaps I, **too, may**
be able **to** express **a** thought **or two in** reference **to the**
sad event which assembles us together.

This blow is one **of the** most appalling which even **my**
long experience can bring **to** mind. It is inconceivable,
almost, that that man, so stalwart in physical proportions,
in strength, cheeriness, cheerfulness, mental, moral and
physical power, can be gone! When the information of
his sickness came to me, I called almost immediately at
his house; and as **I** came **to** his door and there found the
sad emblem of **his death** fluttering **from the bell-handle,**

I could only say "Great God! is this true? How and why?" And what more can we say now? What more ought we to say or do than bow before the wisdom, as well as the power, that has so suddenly bereft us of a friend, and this city of one of its most rising men? We hear a voice as if it spoke to us in two sentences: "Be still and know that I am God," and "What I do thou knowest not now; but thou shalt know hereafter." One thing more we ought to do, which, perhaps, has thus far been omitted; we ought to realize the fact that the consolation in this matter is great, if the blow be great. JOHN P. JACKSON's fate is something about which no Christian man can have a doubt. My friend spoke about the way in which he put away difficulties in theological matters, and went on in simple belief, caring nothing about the disputes that "science, falsely so called," raises against religion. He thus hinted at that which is our consolation and his consolation, and I feel it no more than right, no more than my duty, before the community, before the Bar, to hold up this man as a humble, quiet, unassuming, perhaps reticent, and yet real Christian. He did not know he was to die; he had no dream that his death was so near; but if he had been told it, he would have folded his arms in perfect peace and said, "I know in whom I have believed."

Mr. Chairman, must we not all feel this? and must we not hereafter, as we pass through life — some of us with many years ahead, others with a future which is shortening to their sight every day — must we not, I say, carry this memory along with us, and now and always rejoice, in the contemplation of MR. JACKSON's career, that the Bar of Essex County has furnished to the community a man

universally acknowledged to have been a pattern of true
manliness, and who was known besides, by those who
knew him best, to be a godly, believing, honest and
thorough Christian?

What more can I say?

MR. THOMAS N. McCARTER then said:

MR. CHAIRMAN — I ask the attention of this meeting
for a moment, while I endeavor to add a word to what
has already been said on this occasion. As I did not
grow up with MR. JACKSON, nor commence my professional career in association with him, perhaps I did not
know him so well as some others, but I first became
acquainted with MR. JACKSON in the winter of 1862,
when a very young man. He was a member of the
House of Assembly, of which I was also a member.
It was a very notable House of Assembly, such as this
State seldom sees assembled. It was the second year
of the war, when the people seemed to have but one
mind, and selected their best men to represent them in
our Assembly, and I may mention some gentlemen who
were members of that House besides MR. JACKSON, some
of whom remain and are well known. There were in
that House, Mr. Jacob Vanatta, Socrates Tuttle, George
A. Halsey, John Hill, General Charles Haight, of
Monmouth (who was Speaker), Mr. John Mann, of
Somerville, John G. Stone, of Trenton, and many others,
including our deceased friend; and there I formed his
acquaintance. He could not have been over twenty-five
years of age, and I was struck then with the diligent
and careful attention which he gave to all his duties

as a legislator, and with that patriotic fervor which found him ready to do, without regard to partisan feeling, everything that was necessary to sustain the honor and the safety of our then threatened Government. He was diligent in the discharge of every legislative duty, and without the slightest attempt to make any display or to obtrude himself upon the notice of the Assembly, he was influential in the passage of many important measures which have remained until this day upon our statute-books. I can recall two with which lawyers are familiar, the passage of which was due to his persistent attention and earnest advocacy among the other members. One of them is that statute which permits foreign witnesses to be examined in other States, upon notice, instead of the cumbrous form of taking out a commission, which was introduced and advocated by him, and passed by his exertions. The other is that well-known statute with regard to the protest of promissory notes, which permits notice to be given through the post-office in the same town or city where the endorser lives, thus removing a great difficulty in the proper protesting of notes. I have no doubt that if I took the trouble I could remember a great many more, but those two come under my notice. They all illustrated the fact that he was diligent in the discharge of the duties then cast upon him, and discharged those duties not only with fidelity and prudence, but with great intelligence and zeal. I had also, in addition to that favorable opportunity of making his acquaintance, at the same time an opportunity of meeting him socially in that delightful social circle in Trenton which so many of us enjoyed, and in which he was always welcome because of — and there I first realized and became acquainted with — those beautiful social qualities alluded to here, and for which he was so distinguished. From that time, whenever I met him on the streets of Newark, I was struck with his warm-hearted, generous hospitality. I never met him — when I was coming here — but he invited me to his house and seemed overflowing with that good-nature and kindly feeling which has been referred to here. In after years, when I came to this city and became necessarily acquainted with him in the practice of my profession, I was often pitted against him under circumstances calculated to try the temper and provoke asperity, and I never knew any one more courteous and uniformly kind and polite, even on those occasions when the best of us sometimes give way, and in all our professional intercourse, I cannot recall a single word he uttered that I would wish unsaid. There was not only that gentle courtesy to all around him, but a deferential manner to those who were his seniors in the profession which was beautiful to behold and which could not help but enhance the beauty of his character.

Mr. Jackson would sometimes say in a laughing way, "What is the use of our sitting up nights, bothering ourselves about the law? we have a corps of intelligent judges, well paid to do that; let them look up the law!" But any luckless practitioner who entered into a contest with Mr. Jackson, and supposed he acted on that principle, would find that he *had* looked up the law, and would find, as Mr. Stone suggested, that he was well supplied with those cases which furnished precedents to the occasion. He was a well-balanced man; he did not allow his attention to his profession—in which he never flagged—he did not allow that to freeze out all his social sympathies. He was a broad man; he knew what was going on all over the world; he entertained positive views, and could express himself pleasantly, intelligently on all the ordinary topics of the day; he was interested in all that was going on around him; a member of the Union League Club; but recently President of the Essex County Bible Society; he was active in church and in Sunday-school, and in all their associated enterprises. While he was a lawyer, faithful, diligent, industrious and conscientious, he was not a mere lawyer; but he was a man who partook of everything and enjoyed everything that came in his way.

Above all, Mr. Chairman, he was a wise man; he did not leave until the dying hour the important subject of preparation for death and eternity; nor did he content himself with a mere public profession of religion and then lapse back into indifference or unconcern about that important matter; but he was active in the discharge of every duty belonging to him as a professing Christian, and those who know him best know how faithful he was in his household and in training up his children in the way of truth.

His life was an example to us all; but his death comes to us, especially to those who were his seniors in years, with oh! how sharp a warning, and utters those solemn words, "Be ye also ready: for in such an hour as ye think not, the Son of Man cometh." He was ready, and if this sudden bereavement which has so shocked us shall also have the effect of awakening us, either his seniors or juniors, to the importance of that great concern, then,

great as the calamity seems to us, his death will, **after**
all, be a great blessing. He is gone, Mr. Chairman. **It**
is hard to realize, so sudden has been the shock, and so
unprepared were we all for it. It is hard to realize that
we never shall see his manly form and quick step walking
into this Bar and appearing before this Court; that we
never again shall hear that cheerful, that thrilling voice,
that seemed **to** stir up everybody who came within the
reach of its tones; that we never again shall meet him in
the social circle, around **the** festive board **or** in any of
those places **where he was so** often found and so
universally beloved. But the influence of his example is
with us; the warning that his death has given us is with
us, and we will be **wise** if **we** heed them both; wise if we
cultivate more and more all those beautiful characteristics
and that delightful courtesy and politeness, his chief
charm in professional life; wise if **we** heed the warning
and we ourselves be also ready.

MR. WILLIAM PATERSON then addressed the meet-
ing as follows:

Permit me, **Mr** Chairman, to add a few words to what
has been said **on** this occasion; not, however, with any
idea that I can pay a more worthy tribute to the memory
of the friend who will mingle no longer among us here,
than already has been done. I have known JOHN P.
JACKSON, JR., for half the years he lived on earth, and
most **of** those years, well.

My acquaintance with him commenced at the time to
which reference has been made by that one of our
number who spoke first to the large gathering that

attests the estimation in which Mr. Jackson was held by his professional associates, when he was selected to deliver, on taking the degree of Master of Arts, the oration connected therewith at the college institution where you, sir, and I and many of those present received our early education. He was not of my class in age, and for want of inclination and other qualities not necessary to mention here, the limited legal sphere in which I chose to move was different from the active one in which he participated. Still, I may say that my relations had been more close and intimate with him than with any of those who practice at this Bar, two only excepted. This was professional in part, but to a great extent derived from other causes. The cordiality with which he greeted my appearance among you, now more than thirteen years ago, made an impression upon me lasting to this day, and the whole course of his conduct and bearing since assured me of his sincerity. I have often recalled that act with feelings of gratification and pleasure, the more so as there had been no especial reason why he should have been more marked in that respect than others. But the similarity of interest we felt in promoting the prosperity of the college in which we had been trained was one of the strongest links by which our associations were connected. It was my good fortune, also, to see much of him in the last year or two of the life now terminated so suddenly and sadly, by acting with him on a commission of a public nature, involving many delicate and sensitive interests, requiring the personal attention and intercommunication of each to a large degree, and in considering which I can testify that our friend was faithful and laborious, and second to no other in the thought and time and study he gave to the work he had to prepare.

I have but little more to say. Those of you in Newark here know his character as a citizen and in the relations of private life, and his deportment as a Christian, better than any delineation I could undertake to give. While we differed in many matters and things, as men must continue to do in such a world as this, and while our political views were as variant as well could be, still no divergency of sentiment ever marred the harmony of our intercourse, and all my remembrances of him are only of the kindest and most pleasant nature. I can recall nothing that ever left a smart or a sting, or which he might have wished had not been said. As was his greeting in September, 1867, so were his last words in December, 1880, and so they all had been. It was not among the probabilities in life that I should stand and speak such words as these on an occasion like this, but as the mysterious possibility has occurred which leaves me the survivor of the two, let me assure you that the sentiments I express are sincere in feeling and true in fact.

So our friend, his life and all his labors done, has gone from out the living number here. Who next will pass in turn? Will it be you, or I, or one of those still in their manhood's prime? When the forbidden fruit was taken from the tree of knowledge, the decree went forth that all mankind must die. We know just that; but when or where or how, that we can never know on earth. Like the first parent of the human race, men can look back upon the past. He ate the apple, and memory rose up and threw a backward glance; the present was before him, but the future which he sought to know, that, beyond the certainty of death, was not revealed.

MR. DAVID A. RYERSON then said :

MR. CHAIRMAN — I cannot allow this occasion to pass
without a word for my friend of many years. When I
came to Newark, some twenty years ago, MR. JACKSON
was one of the first to give me welcome. It was a hearty
greeting, warm, generous, strong, and very precious to a
stranger in a strange city. The acquaintance then formed
soon ripened into a friendship that never grew dim, but
was continuous and lasting. And to-day, when I recall
all the pleasant associations we have had together, all his
kindly words and deeds, now seemingly so far away, yet
so golden in memory, the lips fail to utter what the heart
would gladly say.

We all personally feel the loss of this genial, earnest,
noble-hearted man. Some here will recollect the old
Newark Law Club ; an association which, for conscientious
work, harmony of feeling and action, and strong personal
attachments, has probably never been equaled in this city.
It seems to be only a short time ago since we formally
disbanded ; yet the roll-call to-day shows that the majority
of its members have crossed the river — Condit, Haines,
Smith, Perry, Greiner, and now JOHN P. JACKSON, JR.,
with all his manly strength and charm of presence.

His life was full of activity and energy. He was always
ready to do a kindly act ; always cheerful, brave of
purpose, strong in action, pure in thought.

Perhaps it is not for me to speak of, but on an
occasion like this, when the human heart, as well as
revelation, tells us of a life beyond, we cannot help
rejoicing that our brother and friend so lived that

henceforth for him, in a happier clime, there are no more partings, no more tears.

MR. WILLIAM A. RIGHTER then addressed the meeting as follows:

MR. CHAIRMAN — I desire to contribute a word in regard to our departed friend. Others have spoken more of his later life. We have heard interestingly from one who was a student in his office; another who was his partner there; another who was his associate member of the Legislature, and another who has gone with him through all the Courts in this State.

They have displayed his character in such admirable terms that no one can attempt to pass over the ground so thoroughly occupied by them. I desire to call the attention of the young men here to-day to another important feature of his character. When I first came to this city, his learned father and honored mother, whose virtues have been so faithfully sketched by Mr. Stone, received me into the hospitalities of their home; — the homestead at that time was on the west side of Broad street, adjoining the Third Presbyterian Church; and JOHN P. JACKSON was then a school-boy.

I have thus known MR. JACKSON from boyhood — have followed him through his school-days, observed him while in college and in his professional preparation, and also during his professional course — and have had occasion to meet him variously at the Bar, in the street, in business life and in social circles; and I can only emphasize what has been so well said by those who have preceded me — that I never, at any time, heard a word or a suggestion of anything impure or improper from or of MR. JACKSON.

When a youth, he never showed the waywardness and the frivolities which most youths think they cannot escape. He avoided them all; and there was laid the foundation of the great attainments he made.

When a youth, he was always *manly*, and seemed to be constantly entertaining an apprehension that there was before him in life an important place to fill, and to be earnestly preparing for, and pressing forward to, the attainment of that end. It is to this important feature that I desire to call attention, in hopes that it may be impressed upon others, and they induced to emulate and profit by his example.

The foundation must be laid early; correct habits must be formed then; and if they are, there is little danger of that person. The result was that everybody knew they could trust implicitly in John P. Jackson, and that all reliance could be placed upon his word and his honor.

He was always found abiding strictly in honor, purity and truth; and that secured him the estimation, confidence and admiration of this community. And let me say, he did attain to fill a *large place* in this community: —and who, of all this great number here, is prepared to undertake to fill the place of Mr. Jackson? In all the various walks of life he filled a high place, and that was because he was industrious, faithful and true in all its relations.

> "To thine own self be true,
> And it must follow, as the night the day,
> Thou canst not then be false to any man."

4

And thus he was standing always in the right, a
shining example of what it brings to every man. His
whole life seemed a *bounding joy*. We always loved to
meet him everywhere. He was ever welcome, because he
was always cheerful, cheering and ready; prepared for
whatever came to hand; and if I were to mention a
sobriquet peculiarly applicable to him, it would be *semper
paratus*.

As has been said to us, in the church, in the Sunday-
school, in the social circle, at the Bar, in professional
service, in matters of education, research or charity, in
political affairs, he was always ready, prepared to take
his part in each good word and work; to do something —
to be of use.

Is a man's life measured by the number of days he
lives, or by what he accomplishes?

He has fulfilled the high end of showing us how rightly
to live, and that it is within the reach of all, beginning
early, and continuing faithful in well-doing to the end,
to accomplish great good and attain high position.

Of course, nature did much for him in that splendid
physique and in those genial, smiling manners, so rarely
bestowed, and which we shall ever recall with delight;
but his chief merit lay in his fidelity to every trust, in
his conscientious discharge of duty, and in his constant
readiness to do with might whatsoever his hand found to
do. His life was gentle, and the elements so mixed in
him, that Nature might stand up and say to all the
world, "This was a man."

He carried to an untimely grave with him the heartfelt
respect and confidence — yea, the flowing tears — of this
Court, of this Bar, and of this entire community. How

remarkable ! Does it not point, as with the finger of
Eternity, to the couplet :

> " There's a Divinity that shapes our ends,
>   Rough hew them how we will."

The patriarch has put the pertinent question, " If a
man die, shall he live again ? " In this intelligent
audience, after what has been said, I am sure no doubt
can exist on that point. Shall any say this warm heart,
this gentle nature, this ready, active spirit, with all its
capabilities and charms, shall cease to exist, simply because
that bosom heaves no more ?

Is it thinkable that all those aspiring activities shall
perish with the breath of life ? Not to me. It seems
that he has simply passed behind a screen, and a very
thin one. To mortal eyes it is opaque, but to celestial
eyes it is transparent. Don't you think he is standing
just behind now, taking the same interest in the affairs of
life as he did but a few days since ? Can it be otherwise ?
Must we not join him there ? I know we shall. Let us,
then, as we remember how rapidly life brings us near the
same door, ever ajar, strive to emulate his example, and
keep our light burning brightly until the appointed time
comes, when we shall also be called away hence.

> " So live that, when thy summons comes to join
>   The innumerable caravan that moves
>   To that mysterious realm, where each shall take
>   His chamber in the silent halls of death,
>   Thou go not, like the quarry slave at night,
>   Scourged to his dungeon: but, sustained and soothed
>   By an unfaltering trust, approach thy grave
>   Like one who wraps the drapery of his couch
>   About him, and lies down to pleasant dreams."

MR. ELWOOD C. HARRIS then said :

MR. CHAIRMAN — Without **adding** anything **to** what has been so well said, I rise simply to move the adoption of the minute which the Committee has reported to this meeting.

The minute was thereupon unanimously adopted.

SENATOR STONE then said :

MR. CHAIRMAN — Several gentlemen have asked me at what time the committee would **suggest** that members of the Bar should meet here **in** order **to** attend the funeral. The services commence at two o'clock, and we suggest that members **of** the **Bar** meet here **at** half-past one o'clock, which will give **us ample time** to reach the house **in** good season.

The meeting then adjourned.

Proceedings at Princeton College.

——— ✦✦✦ ———

The following paper was read by Rev. William C. Stitt, at Princeton, N. J., on the occasion of the Twenty-fifth Anniversary of the Class of 1856:

JOHN P. JACKSON, JR., was born in Newark, New Jersey, February 6, 1837, and died in Newark, New Jersey, December 17, 1880. He entered college as a Sophomore in 1853, and graduated with the first honor in 1856. In 1857 he entered the Cambridge Law School, and on graduation won a prize for a treatise on Abandonment by the Law of Insurance. In 1859 he was appointed to deliver the Master's Oration at Princeton. He served in the lower house of the Legislature of New Jersey in 1862 and 1863, receiving in the latter year the complimentary nomination for Speaker, when his party was in the minority. He was Counsel for the city of Newark from 1866 to 1870. In 1878 he was before the Convention of the Republican party as a candidate for Congress, but gracefully submitted to its choice of another standard-bearer, and worked hard for his election. At the time of his decease he was a member of the tax commission appointed by the Governor of New Jersey, Trustee of Newark Academy, Secretary of the New Jersey Colonization Society, member of the New Jersey Historical Society and Counsel of the Pennsylvania Railroad.

Our classmate entered life with many advantages, and made the most of them. He inherited a sound mind in a sound body; was reared in a Christian family, by noble parents, received an ample preparation for college, took the head of the class, and kept it by faithful work, and so received the Latin Salutatory, and afterward the Master's Oration, to the satisfaction of the entire class. Had he lived longer, we believe that a high place in his profession and his political life would have been earned by him. As a memorial of his life is in preparation, we must content ourselves here with a classmate's estimate of a classmate.

John P. Jackson's physique was large and noble, his voice ringing and cheerful, his face handsome and intellectual. When he recited, he was so vigorous, manly and attractive that we all looked at him as well as listened to him, and gave the hearty man, as much as the accurate scholar, the meed of our applause. It is not strange that a man of his health and strength should have been a man of genial temperament and spirits. He was happy and sportive among his companions, and his laughter added zest to theirs. Few first-honor men whose honor is won by toil more than by genius ever knew better how to unbend or when to play than our classmate did. Though he never gave to frolic the time that was due to study, no man was ever more ready for mirth than he. He easily won friends and never lost one. He was a "good fellow" among us, as well as our leading scholar, and we all loved him and we all respected him.

As he was our first-honor man in a large class, it goes without saying that his mind was one of unusual powers. To be sure, it was not without labor that he maintained his pre-eminence, but it was not without real ability too.

He clearly grasped all the studies of the course, and maintained a high grade in each of them. We admired the minute accuracy of his recitations, but felt that there was more than the memory of the text-book — there was the power of the thinker.

MR. JACKSON was very genial and gentlemanly in his deportment. I think his position as first-honor man never aroused any envious or dissatisfied feelings in his class or among his rivals and that this fact was due, not only to his merit as a scholar, but also to his own kindly carriage toward all his classmates. His voice and hand and smile made every one his friend, and even his rivals rejoiced in his success.

His character had always been free from any vice, and his moral tone had been pure and high from his childhood. In his Senior year he made a Christian profession, and even for a while earnestly considered the question of entering the ministry.

It was a great joy to hear his pastor at his funeral testify, not only to the qualities which we his classmates knew so well, but also to his Christian fidelity in the family, the Sunday-school and the church. Even the Bar as well as the church gave testimony to his Christian believing and living.

We look upon JOHN P. JACKSON, JR., as a noble specimen of the gentleman, the scholar and the Christian.

His sudden death flings a deep shadow on our meeting to-day. We expected to see his handsome face, to grasp his friendly hand, to hear his hearty voice, but God has called him hence. *Fuit, sed nunc ad astra.*

He was married on the 20th of October, 1868, to Miss Gregory, of Jersey City. Five children survive their father. It is the universal testimony of his kindred and

his friends that he was the kindest husband and father,
and that it was in his family that he expended the wealth
of his generous love, and showed the depth of his religious
affections.

**An extract from the minutes of a meeting of
the** Class **of** 1856, **held in Princeton, September** 21,
1881, **on the occasion of the Twenty-fifth Anniversary of their graduation.**

Another classmate **has** fallen **by the way.** His death
makes the day we celebrate almost painful in memory.

We recall **so** readily, **so** clearly, the man, **the** scholar,
the friend—the pride of our class. Meekly he bore his
honors with the glad consent of us all. **We** were honored
in him who stood twenty-five years ago **the** representative
man of this class. Through these years of **work** and care,
no one has forgotten him, no one ceased **to** honor him,
no one failed to love him. His manly form and bearing, **his** frank **and** genial face, his quick and cordial
manner, his acute and trained intellect ; and above all his
warm and generous heart secured him an imperishable
memory. To-day he is first in our hearts, as twenty-
five years ago he was first in our ranks. While life lasts
and with passing years we renew our fellowship with **the**
living. Amid the hallowed memories of noble **and** useful
lives, **we** will with love and honor cherish the memory
of JOHN P. JACKSON, JR.

Signed by order of the class.

DAVID MAGIE, of *New Jersey*,
W. C. STITT, of **New** *York*,
W. D. HARDEN, of *Georgia*,
S. C. CHEW, of *Maryland*,
G. A. MERCER, of *Georgia*.

Action of the Newark Law Association.

At a meeting of the Newark Law Association, held at their rooms on the 18th day of December, A. D. 1880, the following resolutions were adopted:

WHEREAS, This Association has heard with deep regret and profound sorrow of the decease of JOHN P. JACKSON, JR., ESQ., one of our honorary members; and

WHEREAS, We are desirous of showing our high esteem and respect for the deceased; therefore be it

Resolved, That inasmuch as it has pleased Almighty God, in His all-wise providence, to remove from our midst one whose services in the establishment of this Association we highly appreciate, therefore be it further

Resolved, That we tender to the bereaved family of the deceased our most heartfelt sympathy in their affliction, and that a copy of these resolutions be sent to them, and that the same be also entered upon the minutes of this Association and published in the daily papers. And be it further

Resolved, That we attend the funeral of the deceased.

ARTHUR R. DENMAN.
HOWARD W. HAYES.
FRANK C. WILLCOX.
Committee.

Action of the Republican Association.

Rooms of the Republican Association,
Newark, N. J., Dec. 20, 1880.

At a meeting of the members of the Republican Association, to take action in regard to the late John P. Jackson, Jr., Esq., who, up to the time of his death, was President of the Association,

Vice-President BAKER called the meeting to order and spoke as follows :

GENTLEMEN OF THE REPUBLICAN ASSOCIATION.—It is scarcely necessary for me to say that I deemed it my duty to call you together, in view of the recent sad event with which you are all acquainted, and it is perhaps still more unnecessary for me to recall to you any of the characteristics of the one in whose memory we are assembled. His geniality of disposition and his good-fellowship made him a friend to each and every one of us. Born and reared in Newark, perhaps no man was better known in our community. His abounding health and robust constitution seemed to mark him for one destined to a long life. You all remember as well as I do the interest he took in this Association during the late campaign, and all realize how agreeable his presence made the most monotonous of our committee meetings. I have called you together, gentlemen, to take such action in respect to this loss to the community and this Association as you may deem proper in the premises.

Walter J. Knight was then elected Secretary, and on motion of City Attorney F. S. Fish, the Chair appointed F. S. Fish, Senator Francis, J. L. Sutphen, J. V. Diefenthaeler and James L. Hays a committee to prepare resolutions relative to the death of the late President.

After a brief absence from the meeting, the committee reported the following.

At a meeting of the Republican Association of the City of Newark, convened on the occasion of the death of its President, JOHN P. JACKSON, JR., ESQ., the following declaration was made:

In this sad event there are two sources of feeling—one of profound sorrow at the sudden close of an intimacy so cheerful, useful and honorable as that which MR. JACKSON has maintained with the Association; the other is one of pride and gratitude that a nature so noble as that of our President should have left to us a record so unselfish, so unstained, yet so unfinished; so full of manliness and love to man, so kindly in all its instincts, so brave and positive in all its action, so welded to principle and patriotism, so pure in all its findings, as that of our President.

He stopped on the centre of a life which was cleanly

and devoted to cause. In his entire past there was much
to admire. In his future were bright hopes **of** distinguished
position. Others have spoken their word of his character
as a Christian gentleman and lawyer. **We** speak from a
feeling toward the Republican and the publicist whom we
had chosen as our leader, whom God has pleased to take
from our leadership.

Mr. Jackson **was not a leader** in the common sense of
the **word. He was** as unselfish as he was able and anxious
to direct. Regarding him **as** one of **the** best types of the
true gentleman **and American** citizen, we pay this tribute
to his memory

For ourselves, his **energy, his tact, his** steadfast ways
remain as **a** memory **to be** perpetuated by the man who
must take his **place.**

But to his family we offer the sincere condolence of an
Association in which **he** was destitute of enemies and rich
in friends.

We ask that this minute be spread upon our record,
and that **a** suitable **copy be** engrossed and transmitted to
his family.

These resolutions **were unanimously adopted, and**
the Association then adjourned.

Action of the Newark Academy.

APRIL 21, 1881.

At the annual meeting of the stockholders, held on Tuesday, 19th inst., the President, Samuel H. Pennington, M.D., presented his report, after the reading of which the following resolution was adopted :

Resolved, That the President's Annual Report be accepted and spread upon the minutes, and that so much of it as refers to the late JOHN P. JACKSON, JR., be communicated to his family.

EXTRACT FROM REPORT.

The Trustees would do injustice to their own feelings and the memory of an honored and lamented colleague, were they to conclude this communication without referring, with becoming expressions of esteem and sorrow, to the great loss that, in common with their fellow-citizens, they have suffered in the sudden decease of the late JOHN P. JACKSON, JR.

MR. JACKSON became a member of this board in the year 1869, and, during the whole period of his connection with it, evinced a warm interest in the institution and

the cause of higher education it was designed to promote.
A gentleman of liberal culture and distinguished scholarship, he was well fitted to impart valuable suggestions for
the improvement of the course of study and of the
methods of instruction, and he was at all times as ready
to make, as the board was glad to receive and profit from
them. His intercourse with his colleagues was characterized by cordiality, courtesy and deference; and the
affability and gentlemanly bearing that marked his general
demeanor were equally conspicuous in the deliberations of
the board.

His absence from their councils will be felt and long
lamented, and the cheerful greeting and the warm grasp
with which he was wont to meet his associates will ever be
held by them in affectionate remembrance.

It will devolve on the stockholders at the present
meeting to fill the vacancy created by this afflictive
providence.

They will be fortunate if they make choice of one who
will prove as wise a counselor and as agreeable and
faithful an associate and friend.

[A copy from the minutes.]

CHAS. G. ROCKWOOD,

Secretary.

Obituary Notices.

———— • ————

[*Daily Advertiser, December 18th.*]

DEATH OF JOHN P. JACKSON, JR.

JOHN PETER JACKSON, JR., the well-known lawyer of this city, died at his residence on High street at an early hour last evening, after a few days' illness from a cold, which developed into acute bronchitis. He was attending to his law business in his office, corner Broad and Clinton streets, a week ago, when the heating apparatus got out of order and he contracted his illness. The next day he complained to a friend of pain in the lungs, and on Sunday became worse, so that Dr. O'Gorman was summoned. All the usual remedies failed to arrest the ravages of the disease, which assumed an acute character. Yesterday Dr. Dougherty was called in consultation, and the two physicians expressed the opinion that MR. JACKSON was in a very dangerous condition, and a few hours later he died.

MR. JACKSON was the third son of the late John P. Jackson, the well-known former Vice-President of the

old New Jersey Railroad Company. After a preliminary
education with the late Nathan Hedges, in a class
numbering many of our well-known residents, he entered
Princeton College and graduated in 1856, after which he
took a course in Cambridge Law School, where he received
one of the prizes for the best treatise. On his return to
this city he began the practice of law, and was, until about
a year ago, the partner of ex-Senator Stone, since which
time he has practiced alone. He was a member of the
Legislature in 1862 and 1863, and in the latter year received
the complimentary nomination of the Republican members
for Speaker. He was also City Counsel of this City from
1866 to 1870, under the administration of Mayor Peddie.
Two years ago, MR. JACKSON was prominently named for
member of Congress in this district, and received a
number of votes in the Convention before Mr. Blake was
nominated. He was appointed by Governor McClellan a
member of the Special Commission to frame a general tax
law, whose labors were not yet finished. MR. JACKSON
was also prominently identified with our local politics, and
last spring was elected President of the Newark Republican Association. He frequently spoke at public meetings
throughout the county, and was one of the most active
and earnest Republicans in this community.

MR. JACKSON was also one of the Trustees of the
Newark Academy, Secretary of the New Jersey Coloniza-
tion Society, an active member of the Historical Society,
and connected with other organizations. He was one of
the prominent members of the South Park Presbyterian
Church, and also engaged in the Sunday-school. MR.
JACKSON held a prominent position at the Bar in this
State, and was one of the counsel of the Pennsylvania

Railroad. He married, some years ago, Miss Gregory, of Jersey City, who survives him, with five children. He had a robust physique, and was one of the last persons who would have been selected as likely to succumb early to disease. He was in the forty-fourth year of his age, and was a man of very genial and pleasant manners, which won the love and respect of all with whom he was associated. His death will be sincerely mourned by a large circle of friends all over the State.

MR. JACKSON's last appearance in public was in a legal case on Saturday. He was to have addressed the Board of Trade on tax matters on Wednesday evening, but his place was filled by Prof. Atherton.

The suddenness of MR. JACKSON's death is strongly illustrated in a letter, dated Wednesday last. It is :

NEWARK, Dec. 15, 1880.

Mr. P. T. Quinn :

DEAR SIR—I am confined to my house from the severe effects of the same cold which prevented me from attending your meeting last week. I am glad to read that you expect to hear from Professor Atherton. If you should hold another meeting on this subject before the Tax Commission Bill is acted upon by the next Legislature, I will take pleasure in attending it if you desire.

Yours very sincerely,
JOHN P. JACKSON,
No. 708 High street.

Written only forty-eight hours before his death, there is no evidence of sickness in this casual letter.

[Daily Advertiser, December 18th.]

The sudden **death of JOHN P. JACKSON, JR.**, saddens many a **face to-day and is the** object **of a** shocked surprise. **He was so** stalwart **in** form, so cheerful in temper, **so hardy in all his** ways, that a long life seemed assured to him. **All the other** elements seemed to combine in his favor. **He loved** work and **he** loved recreation, never letting the **one interfere** with the other. With **a** keen sense of duty and a **manly** industry in the affairs **of life, he** combined a joyous **liking** for society, which **showed** itself at home, **in** the office or **on** the street. On **the** street, his eye **was** quick **and** alert, and his salute **was** as graceful as it was resonant and manly. Somewhat ambitious of political preferment, especially for a nomination to Congress **only** three short months ago, he gave no sign of disappointment, and confirmed his chances of a future success by **a** cordial and sincere effort to do his best in every way. **He** was **a** brave soldier, a trusted lawyer, happy in all his relations — the most sacred as well as the most public — full of friendships, incapable of enmities, Christian and therefore gentleman. But for him the laughing day is done before he felt the slightest sense of that weariness **of** life which is the sorrow and disappointment of so many.

[*Evening Journal, December 18th.*]

THE DEATH OF MR. JACKSON.

Under any circumstances, the death of MR. JOHN P.
JACKSON, JR., would arouse a deep and wide-spread
feeling in this community; but under those attending his
demise, so sudden, so surprising and so startling, we do
not wonder that the public is shocked and can scarcely
realize the truth of the lamentable occurrence. Aside
from his highly respectable and even distinguished family
relations, MR. JACKSON was greatly esteemed, not only
among those who enjoyed intimacy with him, but among
those who had merely a passing acquaintanceship with
him. His handsome person, polished address and most
genial manner and gentlemanly ways won for him
everywhere a cordial and kindly reception. Thousands in
this community who scarcely knew the man to speak to
him have learned of his death to-day with feelings akin
to those that would possess them in the event of a personal
bereavement. Never was the uncertainty of life so
strikingly illustrated as in this event which gives every
one pause. But yesterday, we might say, this man of
splendid physique was in our midst, bearing his full share
of the work of life, presenting an appearance of perfect
health, and with every prospect before him of reaching a
ripe old age. To-day he lies stark and stiff in the
undertaker's casket, the victim of a miserable cold which,
at their peril, as we are now so terribly warned, ninety-

nine people out of every hundred treat with comparative contempt. Verily, verily, **the** beautiful burial service of the Book **of** Common **Prayer** reminds **us** —

In the midst of **life we are in** death.
Earth to earth, **ashes** to ashes, dust to dust.

To the family **bereaved with such** dreadful suddenness **we tender** our sincere **and** heartfelt sympathy, a sentiment **in** which **our** readers, **we** feel sure, will unite with **us.**

Extract from a memorial of JOHN P. JACKSON (who died December 10, 1861), father of JOHN P. JACKSON, JR.

MR. JACKSON was born at Aquackanock, in the year 1805, and graduated at Princeton College at an early age, taking the highest honor. He immediately entered upon the study of the law, pursuing his studies at the old Litchfield Law School. In the spring of 1827 he was admitted to practice at the Bar. Shortly after, he became connected with the New Jersey Railroad. Few men in the State have filled larger spheres of usefulness than MR. JACKSON. His father was the late Peter Jackson, who was known in former times, both in New York and New Jersey, as a successful merchant. The Jackson family are of Scotch-Irish descent. Its first emigrant to this country was James Jackson, who, in the year 1746 settled on the banks of the Hudson.

The maternal ancestors of MR. JACKSON were Dutch, and the names of Brinckerhoff, Schuyler and Van-Der-Linde, borne by the highly respectable and pious Hollanders who emigrated hither in the last century, are found in his direct lineage, within the third degree upward.

Extract from a memorial of MRS. ELIZABETH WOLCOTT JACKSON (who died October 15, 1875), mother of JOHN P. JACKSON, JR.

MRS. JACKSON was a native of Litchfield, Conn., a village long since distinguished for its social, educational and religious advantages. The great-grandfather of MRS. JACKSON, Major-General Roger Wolcott, was the first Governor of Connecticut. Her grandfather was Oliver Wolcott, Sr., a signer of the Declaration of Independence. Her uncle, Oliver Wolcott, Jr., was Secretary of the Treasury under General Washington. Her father was Frederick Wolcott, who occupied judicial positions for forty years in his native State. Her mother was a Huntington, and intimately connected with a long line of distinguished citizens.

ERRATUM.

Page 4, eighth line, should read *Secretary* and Member of the Executive Committee of the Essex County Bible Society, instead of *President*.